I Am
Helen Keller

By Grace Norwich

Illustrated by
Mark Elliot

SCHOLASTIC INC.

All rights reserved. Published by Scholastic Inc. SCHOLASTIC and associated logos are trademarks and/or registered trademarks of Scholastic Inc.

ISBN 978-0-545-44779-9

10 9 8 7 6 5 4 3 2   13 14 15 16 17/0

Printed in the U.S.A.   40
First printing, October 2012

Cover illustration by Mark Fredrickson
Interior illustrations by Mark Elliot
Book design by Kay Petronio

Contents

Introduction 4

People You Will Meet 8

Time Line 10

Chapter One: An Ordinary Start 12

Chapter Two: Same Kid, New World 18

Chapter Three: Annie's Arrival 24

Chapter Four: Teaching Helen 34

Chapter Five: Every Word, a Thought 42

Chapter Six: Still a Lot to Learn 50

Chapter Seven: Off to the Big City 60

Chapter Eight: Next Stop, College 66

Chapter Nine: Ivy—League Girl 72

Chapter Ten: An Unlikely Love Story 80

Chapter Eleven: Helen Speaks Up 86

Chapter Twelve: Helen's Name in Lights 96

Chapter Thirteen: Fairwell, Teacher 102

Chapter Fourteen: Fighting to the End 110

10 Things You Should Know About
    Helen Keller 114

10 MORE Things That Are Pretty Cool to Know . 118

Glossary 122

Places to Visit 124

Bibliography 126

Index 128

Introduction

I was the most famous child in the world because I learned to read, write, and even speak despite the fact that I was deaf and blind. People think my existence was a dark, soundless prison. That's just not true.

Life is more than color and sound; I felt the world.

My senses of smell and touch were super-human. Not only did I feel a pencil rolling off a table or a passing airplane thousands of feet in the sky while inside a house, but I could tell who was in the room below me by the particular vibrations of their steps. I smelled storms before they came, and I recognized what people did for a living by the scents on their clothes. Carpenters smelled of wood, doctors of sickness, and schoolteachers of chalk. You'd be surprised by how much is missed when you only look at a

flower instead of touching and smelling it.

I shocked a lot of folks when I smiled at them as they walked into the room. But of course, it's no miracle that I could recognize people I had met before. I smelled and felt their presence a mile away. Still, many acted like those abilities were gifts God gave me for being an angel. Believe me, I was no angel. I had a terrible temper at times and was known for being very stubborn. Plus, I spent *a lot* of money on fancy clothes and fancy dogs. What angel does that?

It actually hurt my feelings when others insisted that I was always "sweet and earnest." More than anything else, I wanted to be an ordinary girl and take part in what I called "the everyday nothings of life."

What made me extraordinary was my firm belief that all of us, no matter our abilities, have the right to an education, to do work that's interesting, and to make friends we like. That's what I spent my entire life fighting for.

"I wish I might be taken just as a normal person," I wrote, "and my accomplishments treated simply as illustrations of how much more others can do if they only use their five senses with thought and perseverance."

I became one of the most famous Americans of all time because I never let my eyes and ears keep me from having a wonderful life. For someone who was blind, I sure could see a lot. I am Helen Keller.

People You Will Meet

HELEN KELLER:
When a severe illness left her completely blind and deaf, Helen learned to read and write, then spent her life fighting for the rights of disabled people all over the world.

CAPTAIN ARTHUR KELLER:
Helen's father, a strict southern gentleman who adored his daughter and would have done anything for her, but wasn't always able to because of his severe debt.

KATE KELLER:
Fiercely protective, Helen's mother was sometimes unsure about her daughter's close relationship with Annie, but she knew that the amazing teacher made everything in Helen's life possible.

ANNIE SULLIVAN:
After showing Helen the meanings of words and unlocking the outside world to her, Teacher (as Helen called her) never left her grateful pupil's side.

MICHAEL ANAGNOS:
The director of the Perkins Institution for the Blind made Helen's name famous by publicizing her achievements to the rest of the world—sometimes exaggerating them in the process.

JOHN ALBERT MACY:
A young Harvard English professor who, while helping Helen with her writing, fell in love with Annie.

POLLY THOMSON:
Hired in 1914 to help Helen and Annie organize their increasingly busy schedules, the Scottish woman became one of Helen's lifelong companions.

PETER FAGAN:
A secretary who helped during one of Helen's speaking tours; he and Helen fell in love and wanted to marry, but the Keller family shunned him and put a stop to the romance.

Time Line

June 27, 1880

Helen Keller is born in Tuscumbia, Alabama.

1882

Helen loses her hearing and sight after a terrible illness.

1887

Annie Sullivan arrives at Helen's home to become her teacher.

August 19, 1896

Helen's father, Captain Keller, passes away.

1900

Helen enters the freshman class of Radcliffe College.

1903

Helen publishes *The Story of My Life*.

1904

Helen graduates from Radcliffe, becoming the first deaf–blind person to receive that type of college degree.

1920

Helen and Annie become vaudeville performers.

1921

Helen's mother, Kate Keller, passes away.

October 20, 1936

Annie passes away.

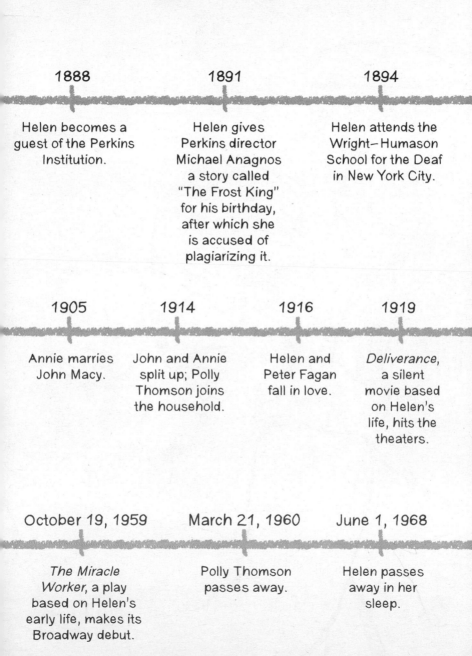

1888
Helen becomes a guest of the Perkins Institution.

1891
Helen gives Perkins director Michael Anagnos a story called "The Frost King" for his birthday, after which she is accused of plagiarizing it.

1894
Helen attends the Wright–Humason School for the Deaf in New York City.

1905
Annie marries John Macy.

1914
John and Annie split up; Polly Thomson joins the household.

1916
Helen and Peter Fagan fall in love.

1919
Deliverance, a silent movie based on Helen's life, hits the theaters.

October 19, 1959
The Miracle Worker, a play based on Helen's early life, makes its Broadway debut.

March 21, 1960
Polly Thomson passes away.

June 1, 1968
Helen passes away in her sleep.

CHAPTER ONE

An Ordinary Start

Helen Keller came into the world on June 27, 1880, like anybody else. She was the first daughter of proud parents Kate and Arthur Keller. Everyone called Helen's father Captain because he had fought in the **Confederate** army during the Civil War. A quiet and serious man, Captain did lots of different things, including training as a lawyer, planting cotton, and editing a newspaper called the *North Alabamian*.

Helen's mom, Kate Adams Keller, was related to John Adams, a founding father of the country and the second president of the United States of America.

John Adams

At six months old, Helen proved she was a smart kid. She could already say a few words, like *tea* and *water*. Her parents doted on her as she grew, and soon she was a happy, energetic toddler running around her big home in Tuscumbia, Alabama, called Ivy Green.

When Helen was nineteen months old, she became very, very sick. Kate and Arthur quickly called the doctor, who diagnosed her as having "brain fever." Helen probably came down with scarlet fever or meningitis, two serious illnesses that are now often curable with antibiotics. The **penicillin** to treat her fever, however, wasn't invented until almost sixty years later, so her parents and doctor couldn't do anything except worry. Everyone thought Helen was going to die, but after a few days her fever went down and she seemed, by some miracle, to have recovered.

Visit Helen's Birthplace

If you are ever in Alabama, you can visit Ivy Green, which is just as it was when Helen was alive. The white clapboard home on 640 acres was built in 1820 and got its name from the English ivy that winds itself around the house, fences, and surrounding magnolia trees. For more information, go to helenkellerbirthplace.org.

Only she was no longer the same little girl. It didn't take long after Helen felt better for Kate to notice something wasn't right. She passed her hand in front of her daughter's eyes and saw that Helen didn't blink. That wasn't

all. When the dinner bell rang loudly enough to send people from all over the large house to the dining room, Helen didn't flinch or even look up. In a panic, Kate rattled one of Helen's favorite toys, a tin can with stones in it, but still no reaction. Captain clapped and called to his baby. Nothing.

The illness had left Helen deaf and blind.

Same Kid,
New World

Helen was now blind and deaf, but she still had lots of energy and curiosity as she explored Ivy Green. Inside, she rushed around, holding on to her mother's skirts. Outside, she used the walls of the house as a guide, touching everything that grew on the lush property.

She had the normal likes and dislikes of any kid, but she couldn't communicate them to anyone else. Even more frustrating, Helen could feel others moving their lips, vibrations

coming out, and then people responding to those vibrations. Yet, when she moved her lips, nothing happened.

Upset and confused, Helen would often throw major tantrums, especially when she didn't get her way. She scratched, bit, smashed plates, and threw things until pure exhaustion got her to stop. "I have a naughty temper," she later wrote. "I am stubborn, impatient."

Helen's parents didn't know how to help.

They felt bad for Helen, so they let her do pretty much anything she wanted. (If they didn't, instant tantrum time!) That included walking around the table during meals and sticking her fingers in other people's food to fish out her favorite morsels.

Strong-willed and smart, Helen developed her own version of sign language in order to communicate. By the time she was five, she had invented fifty signs, including one for every member of her family. (Patting her cheek symbolized her mother; for her dad she pretended to put on glasses.)

Helen had the basics down, but there was so much more than food and family to talk about. How could she make sense of new emotions—like the jealousy she felt when her new sister, Mildred, was born—if she couldn't express them? Anger seemed to be the only way available. It wasn't long after Mildred's

Helen's Own Language

ACTION	MEANING
making the cranking motion of an ice-cream machine handle and pretending to shiver	ice cream
come	pull
go	shove
pinching a little bit of the skin on her hand	smalll
spreading her fingers wide and putting her hands together	large
pretending to cut a slice of bread and buttering it	bread

arrival when Helen decided to do something about this annoying creature, who took up a lot of her mother's attention. She turned Mildred's cradle over to dump her on the floor. Kate caught Mildred just before she fell, but it was now clear they had to stop Helen before she hurt herself or someone else.

Should they send Helen to live in an institution, which was a common practice at that time for children born with differences? Helen's parents wanted their little girl at home but worried about what she was capable of. Helen's aunt Evaline thought she knew the answer: "This child has more sense than all the Kellers—if there is any way to reach her mind." The Kellers needed a teacher.

CHAPTER
THREE

Annie's Arrival

When Annie Sullivan got off the six-thirty train in Tuscumbia, she was so tired and excited she could hardly walk the few short steps to meet the carriage waiting to take her back to Ivy Green. Everyone was nervous on that fateful day in March 1887. Kate and Captain hoped this twenty-year-old recent graduate could get through to their daughter.

The Kellers had begun their quest to find Helen help about a year earlier, when they

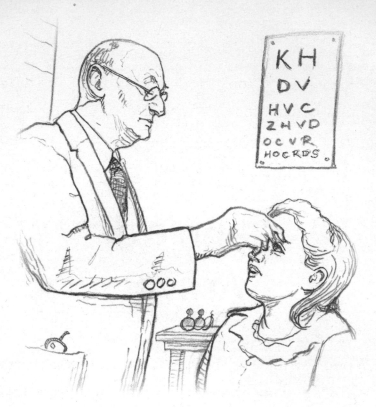

visited an eye doctor in Baltimore. Although nothing could be done to fix Helen's eyes, the doctor suggested the family visit Alexander Graham Bell in nearby Washington, D.C. That's right, the same guy who invented the telephone in 1876! Dr. Bell was deeply interested in the troubles of deaf people because his mother and wife were deaf.

The Kellers took the doctor's advice and paid the famous inventor a visit. Helen and Dr. Bell immediately liked each other. Having climbed on his lap, Helen touched Dr. Bell's big bushy beard. In turn, Dr. Bell gave Helen his watch, with its interesting vibrations, to play with. He told Kate and Captain that they should contact the Perkins Institution, a famous school for

Alexander Graham Bell

Throughout his life, Dr. Bell remained friends with Helen and was committed to helping other deaf–blind people. He founded the American Association to Promote Teaching of Speech to the Deaf, and contributed $25,000 to the organization.

the deaf and blind, for help. About forty years earlier, a deaf-blind girl named Laura Bridgman had learned to read, write, and use sign language at the school. There was hope for Helen!

A Teacher Is Born

Born to poor Irish immigrants in Massachusetts, Annie Sullivan had a very rough childhood. When Annie was only eight, her mother died, leaving her and her little brother, Jimmie, with their alcoholic father, who couldn't take care of them. So they were sent to the poorhouse, a dirty and scary place filled with criminals, sick people, and the poor, all mixed together. Not long after they arrived, Jimmie died of tuberculosis. If that wasn't enough, Annie suffered from an eye infection that went untreated and left her vision permanently hazy and blurry.

Annie could have easily given up, but that wasn't her personality. She was headstrong and, like Helen, had a quick temper. She

wasn't going to go down without a fight. While the chairman of the State Board of Charities, a very important man, was visiting the poorhouse one day, a fourteen-year-old Annie followed him around, making sure to quietly stay out of the way. When the man, who Annie could only detect by his large dark shape and nice accent, was about to leave, she made her move.

"I want to go to school!" she said loudly.

Her bold plan worked and the chairman was moved to send her to Perkins, where Annie got a top-notch education and turned out to be one of the school's smartest students. After an operation restored her vision, she graduated first in her class in 1886.

The Kellers immediately sent a letter to Perkins, because they were fortunate enough to be able to pay for a teacher to come live with them.

The school agreed and chose Annie for the job.

Helen waited on the porch of Ivy Green for whatever was happening to happen. She knew something was up—everyone had been cleaning and cooking furiously for days—but she didn't know what it was. By the time Helen felt the vibrations of the carriage barreling down the country road, a small group of neighbors had arrived to watch the action. Helen sensed slow, light steps up the porch and toward her, an unfamiliar smell of strong soap, and then a sturdy pair of arms hugging her.

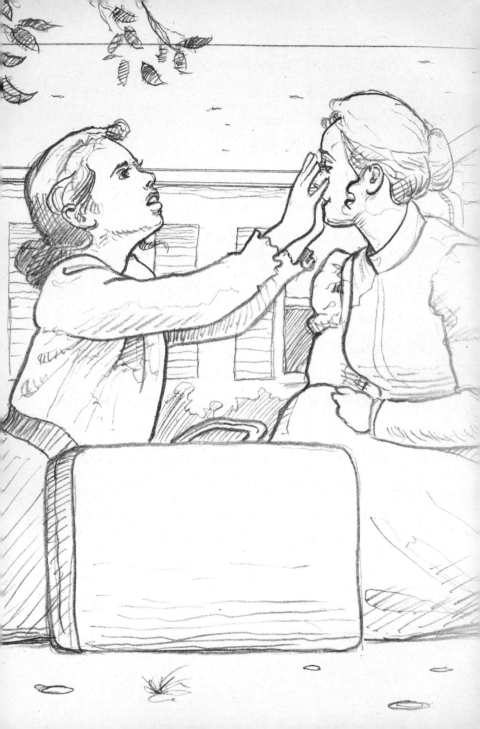

CHAPTER FOUR

Teaching Helen

For Annie's first job out of school, this was a hard one. It was going to take a lot of work to teach Helen how to communicate, but she would never succeed if she didn't first deal with her student's bad behavior.

Annie got a taste of Helen's temper from the first moment they met. After Helen touched the face and dress of this new person, she found the stranger's bag and tried to open it in search of treats. Except Annie's bag was locked. Helen

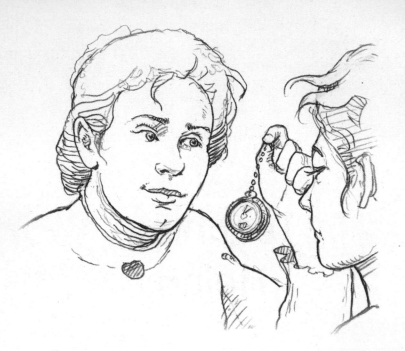

made the motion of turning a key, but Annie took the bag away. That sent Helen into a rage where she kicked her legs like a mule. Annie calmed down the little girl by putting her watch to Helen's face. The ticking made her forget how mad she was, but it wouldn't always be so easy to control her.

At breakfast in the Keller house, Annie was shocked watching Helen make her usual rounds to everyone's food. Annie refused to let her eat from her plate, which sent Helen into a fit. The young teacher had dealt with way worse things than a little girl's tantrum. She wasn't going to let this get the best of her.

Everyone else left the table. Then Annie entered into a huge test of wills with Helen, who turned out to be just as stubborn as she was.

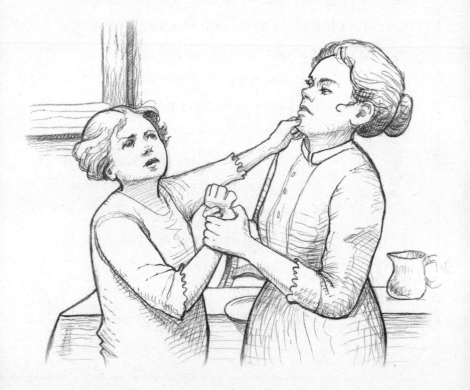

Helen's First Lesson

Helen was brought to Annie's room while the teacher unpacked her trunk. As Annie removed her few possessions from the bag, Helen found a doll made by the girls at Perkins with clothes sewed by Laura Bridgman, the deaf–blind woman who had learned to read and write many years before. Deciding there was no time like the present to start her lessons, Annie slowly spelled *d–o–l–l* into Helen's hand. Then Annie put Helen's hand over hers as she pointed to the doll. After, she made Helen feel her face while she nodded. Annie knew pointing and nodding was Helen's sign for ownership. Misunderstanding that Annie meant to take the doll for herself, Helen had one of her famous tantrums. Annie kept trying to spell

the word, but Helen was too angry to learn anything. Annie needed to get Helen out of her bad mood.

Annie ran downstairs, got a piece of cake, and brought it up to Helen. She spelled the word *cake* into Helen's hand and then gave her the treat. With Helen too busy stuffing her face with cake to be angry, Annie brought out the doll and spelled the word again. Helen repeated the motion of the letters *d–o–l* for Annie, who made the last *l* and then gave the doll to the girl.

The teacher insisted that the girl not only eat her own food, but also do it using a spoon. The battle got so bad that Helen pinched Annie and Annie wound up slapping Helen. Annie finally got her way—Helen ate her breakfast with a spoon—but after the meal, Annie went to her room and cried.

Annie recognized that she had to change Helen's bad habits if she was going to help her interact with the world. Helen had to listen to, bond with, and trust Annie. To do that, Annie had to separate her from Kate and Captain, who couldn't bear to say no to their daughter ever—even when it wasn't good for her.

There was a little cottage on the property that Annie decided she and Helen would move into. First they changed around the furniture, so Helen wouldn't recognize it. Then Captain drove the teacher and his daughter around in circles before arriving at the  cottage, so it seemed like they had traveled some distance.

It took two long weeks, during which the Kellers could hear the horrible sounds of their daughter screaming and objects breaking, but Annie finally got through to Helen. "My heart is singing for joy this morning. A miracle has happened!" Annie wrote. "The light of understanding has shown upon my little pupil's mind, and behold, all things are changed! The wild little creature of two weeks ago has been transformed into a gentle child."

CHAPTER
FIVE

Every Word,
a Thought

With their rough start behind them, Annie and Helen settled into a nice routine of sewing, exercising outdoors, and learning to spell new words using the manual alphabet. Helen was a quick learner, and by the end of a month she could spell eighteen nouns and three verbs. Although she mastered the shapes that made letters, Helen still didn't understand the fundamental connection between words and communication. She didn't know that the motions Annie made into her hand represented things in real life

April 5, 1887, was like any ordinary day, with Annie continuing to show Helen new words. While they were washing up, Helen wanted to know what the cold stuff falling on her hands was, so Annie spelled the word. Helen gave her teacher the same blank stare she always did; she still couldn't make the connection.

A Very Brief History of Sign Language

5th Century BC

Socrates, an ancient Greek philosopher, advocated for deaf people to communicate using their hands, heads, or any other body part that made sense.

1520–1584

Pedro Ponce de Léon, a Spanish monk often called "the first teacher for the deaf," created a system of movements to educate his deaf students.

Late 1700s

Abbé de l'Epée founded the National Institution for Deaf–Mutes in France, which was the first school to teach the deaf. (Most deaf children until that point had private teachers.)

1808

Abbé Sicard, who was director of the National Institution in France after de l'Epée, created a dictionary of hand signs so that hearing and deaf people could understand one another.

What Is the Manual Alphabet?

Each hand shape in the manual alphabet corresponds to a written letter in the English alphabet. (The deaf–blind manual alphabet is slightly different than the one used for people who are only deaf.)

A

B

C

D

E

F

G

H

I

J

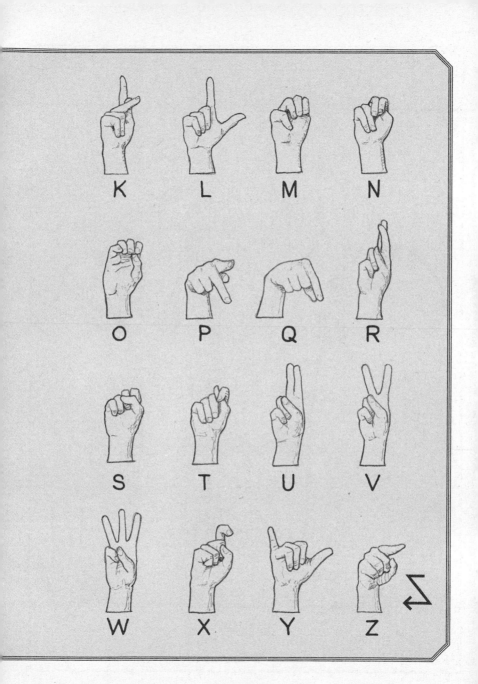

K   L   M   N

O   P   Q   R

S   T   U   V

W   X   Y   Z

47

Suddenly, Annie had an idea. She led Helen to the water pump outside and poured liquid over the little girl's hands, all the while spelling the word into them over and over. Annie searched Helen's face until it shifted from blank to bright. Helen *understood*. "She has learned that everything has a name," Annie wrote, describing the moment. "And each name gave birth to a new thought," Helen later wrote in her **autobiography**.

Within a few hours, Helen had dozens of new words in her vocabulary. She asked the names of everything around her—the pump, the ground, and finally, Annie. *T-e-a-c-h-e-r*, Annie spelled after the young girl touched her face.

Helen would never forget how Annie opened up the entire universe to her. "My spirit was indeed in prison before my teacher came to me," Helen wrote. "But her love and the power of knowledge set me free."

CHAPTER
SIX

Still a Lot
to Learn

A few weeks after her breakthrough, Helen had learned a hundred words. Another month went by, and she learned a hundred more. By June she had four hundred words in her vocabulary that ranged from *mattress* to *maple sugar*. It was time for Helen to move on to braille, the system of raised dots on paper that allows the blind to read, and be introduced to what would become a lifelong passion: books.

From the moment she started work, Annie

What Is Braille?

In 1824, a blind Frenchman named Louis Braille met a soldier who had created something he called night writing. The soldier's system of raised dots was supposed to let soldiers read important messages and instructions at night without a light. But it was way too complicated, so no one ever used it. Louis refined the system and published the first braille book when he was just twenty years old. Today braille is used all over the world in almost every language.

kept the director of the Perkins Institution up-to-date on Helen's progress. The director, Michael Anagnos, wrote about it in his report on the school, taking an amazing story and perhaps making it a little *too* amazing. The press took the news and made it even more incredible. When Annie read a *Boston Herald* item about Helen, she was shocked that it described her student as being able to talk

Some of the Exaggerations Printed about Helen:

- understood seven languages
- educated herself
- recognized colors by touch
- predicted rain
- was never sad or discouraged

fluently, when at most she could put two or three words together at a time. That was just the beginning. Soon, newspapers all over the country called Helen the "wonder child."

The press and the public loved to hear about Helen because her story was so hopeful and positive. She showed everyone how much a deaf-blind girl could do. By 1888 Helen had become one of the most famous children in the country and even received fan mail. That spring, Helen was invited to meet President Grover Cleveland!

Helen loved the attention and used it for a good cause: to raise money for other deaf-blind kids who weren't as lucky to come from families with money like she had. But Annie, fiercely protective of Helen, wasn't so sure about all the **publicity**. Despite Annie's worries, reporters

Helen Finds Her Voice

While in Boston to study at Perkins, Helen insisted on speaking lessons after hearing that a deaf–blind girl in Norway had learned to talk. (Helen could already lipread, which she did by feeling the air that came out of the speaker's nose and the vibrations of the speaker's lips.) To learn what sounds to make for different letters, she put her hands inside her teacher's mouth to feel what her tongue and lips were doing. Sometimes when she practiced with Annie, Helen made Annie gag. She did learn to speak, but never completely clearly.

continued to follow
Helen's every move,
including her trip to
the White House and
later to the Perkins
Institution in Boston.

Helen enjoyed her celebrity,
but soon she experienced the other, harsher
side of fame. In 1891 an eleven-year-old Helen
wrote a story about a kingdom of snow for
Michael Anagnos, who had been so kind to let
her come to the school, in honor of his birthday.
The director loved "The Frost King" so much
that he printed it in his school report, which
of course was reprinted in a newspaper. That
would have been just fine, except it turned
out Helen's story was almost identical to "The
Frost Fairies" by Margaret T. Canby. Soon the
columns about Helen were no longer positive
but instead scandalous. She was accused of

plagiarism, which means stealing someone else's writing and pretending it's your own.

Helen admitted to making a mistake, but swore she didn't remember reading the original story. It's possible she'd heard it long ago and when she sat down to write her own story, the words came out from a deep part of her excellent memory.

The director, who was embarrassed about the incident, made Helen go before a jury of Perkins officials, who eventually decided she was innocent. The bad press, however, couldn't be reversed. Just as quickly as the fan mail had started coming, it stopped. The entire incident left Helen lonely and afraid of making the same mistake.

CHAPTER SEVEN

Off to the Big City

In the fall of 1894, when Helen was fourteen years old, she and Annie set off for New York City. What was a deaf-blind girl from the South doing in a big, crazy (and back then, very smelly) city like Manhattan? Pursuing Helen's never-ending quest to learn.

Helen was in New York to attend the Wright-Humason School for the Deaf, where she would take a full course load including math, English, American history, French, and German. That was in addition to working on her lipreading and speaking skills! That was a lot of work, even for someone as smart as Helen. But she was determined to get through the high-school courses that would prepare her for college.

Helen insisted she was going to college.

That was a pretty outrageous claim, even for someone as exceptional as Helen. Most women didn't go to college in those days, let alone deaf-blind ones. As if that goal wasn't challenging enough, she set her sights on the women's college with the best reputation in the country: Radcliffe, Harvard's sister school. Though it seemed like a dream to most people, Helen believed she could do anything a hearing and seeing girl could.

There was one problem, however. Money. And Helen and Annie didn't have any.

Although the Kellers had once been a **prominent** family, for the last several years before his death in 1896, Captain had huge debts. He hadn't paid Annie to teach Helen for years.

If Helen and Annie worried about how they were going to pay for Wright-Humason or college, they didn't show it while in New York,

64

where they lived like rich ladies. That's because very wealthy people, like John D. Rockefeller, became Helen's benefactors, which means they gave her money so she could continue to study. They paid for school, a nice house, and daily horseback rides in Central Park for both Helen and Annie.

Helen had the time of her life in New York. She went to the dog show at Madison Square Garden because she and Annie loved fancy breeds of dogs. Helen even went to the top of the Statue of Liberty.

CHAPTER
EIGHT

Next Stop, College

New York was a great experience, but if Helen was really going to get into Radcliffe, she needed to go to a school that was even harder than Wright-Humason. She needed to go to a school for hearing girls.

Again Helen set her sights on one of the top prep schools in the country, the Cambridge School for Young Ladies in Massachusetts. At first, the headmaster, Arthur Gilman, had been worried about admitting Helen. He wasn't sure she'd be able to keep up with the difficult curriculum. But Helen proved any fears totally unfounded when she aced her first year at the demanding school. In fact, she did so well, the school said she could graduate early.

It was hard work, especially for Annie, who had to sign teachers' lectures into Helen's hand as they spoke, as well as translate entire books they couldn't get in braille by manual alphabet. This proved especially difficult for Annie since she didn't know French, German, or Latin, so she had to learn the subjects while signing them for Helen.

Unfortunately, Helen's second year was an academic bust, mainly because of math, which even with her determination and smarts she just couldn't seem to grasp. The stress and strain on Annie and Helen was clear to everyone, including Headmaster Gilman. Teachers were complaining to him that Annie

was too hard on Helen. He wrote to Helen's mom that he thought Annie was harming her daughter and the two should be separated. So far away from the school, Kate worried about her daughter. Trusting the headmaster, she named him Helen's legal guardian to do what he thought best.

When Annie was told to leave the school, Helen became hysterical. First she sobbed uncontrollably, then she went on a hunger strike. The situation got so bad that Kate finally had to travel from Alabama. After seeing the situation for herself, she completely changed her mind and accused Headmaster Gilman of being the one to harm her daughter. Teacher and Helen would never be separated again.

CHAPTER NINE

Ivy–League Girl

After finishing her high-school studies with a private tutor, Helen passed her college entrance exams and in 1900 became the first deaf-blind person in the country to attend college. And not just any old college: Helen achieved her goal of making it into Radcliffe!

Wanting something is one thing, and getting it is another. Once at Radcliffe, the classes were so hard, they made the Cambridge school seem like kindergarten. They worked as they had before, with Annie translating the professors' lectures in class. With only a high-school education herself, Annie now had to interpret lessons from instructors at the top college in the country. She struggled to understand the meaning of their words just as fast as she put them into Helen's hands. Between the classes and spelling out the big academic books, Annie was totally exhausted.

Meanwhile, even with Annie's help, Helen faced challenges. She couldn't take notes during lectures, because her hands were busy listening to Annie's translation. So when she got back to her room, Helen had to type everything she could remember on her braille computer. She couldn't even complain to her fellow classmates. None of them knew the manual alphabet, which meant their interactions didn't go much further than "Hello" and "How are you?" "A sense of isolation enfolds me like a cold mist as I sit alone," she wrote about that time.

Although she was already cramming day and night to keep up, Helen decided to take on an added assignment. During her sophomore year of college, she was asked by *Ladies' Home Journal* to write a series of articles about her life. Although handling a professional writing gig on top of her schoolwork seemed impossible,

Helen couldn't say no—in part because they offered her $3,000 for the articles! That was a fortune back then.

It probably won't come as a surprise that the **editors** sent back her first article because it wasn't any good. There was a long list of complaints. It rambled on without any point, jumping around in time, making no sense, and sometimes leaving out important information. Just as she received the harsh criticism, the editors were already sending urgent telegrams saying they needed the next article . . . right away! As Helen put it herself, she was in "deep water."

Friends of Helen and Annie recommended they hire John Albert Macy, a young Harvard English professor and editor of *Youth's Companion*, a popular children's magazine, to shape her ideas into professional pieces. Not only did John fix her articles so that *Ladies'*

Home Journal was proud to run them, but he also came up with the idea to string all the articles together into a **memoir**. The end result was *The Story of My Life*, published to great reviews in 1903, when Helen was just a twenty-two-year-old college junior.

Helen's Books

The Story of My Life was just the first of a long list of books written by Helen. Here are some of her other titles.

- *Out of the Dark*
- *The World I Live In*
- *My Religion*
- *Midstream: My Later Life*
- *Teacher: Anne Sullivan Macy*

Helen graduated from college on June 28, 1904, as the first deaf-blind person in the country to earn a bachelor of arts degree.

An Unlikely
Love Story

John not only helped Helen become a published
author, he also fell in love with Annie. He asked
her to marry him many times, but she refused
him over and over. She might have worried
about the fact that he was more than ten years
younger than her. For sure, she was nervous
about what a marriage might mean for Helen's
future. The two were closer than sisters. In the
end, Annie made John ask Helen's permission.
When he did, he assured Helen that she would

live with them and nothing between her and
Annie would change. Even if it had to change,
Helen gave her wholehearted blessing. She
wanted her beloved teacher to be happy.

John was true to his word. After he and
Annie were married in 1905, the three of them

settled down in the Wrentham, Massachusetts, farmhouse that Annie and Helen had bought together earlier. This could have easily been an awkward arrangement, but it turned out to be "a bit of heaven," Helen wrote. The warm home was always filled with good food, fresh flowers, and dear friends. John helped Helen with the writing she did in her cozy new study. He put ropes along the fields so that Helen could take walks by herself around the property. And he also introduced her to politics.

John, a member of the Socialist Party of America, which was popular in the early twentieth century, introduced Helen to the writings of Communism's founder, Karl Marx, and other radical thinkers of the time. Although Annie didn't approve, Helen took up John's views and joined the Socialist Party. She also joined the suffrage movement that fought to give women the right to vote.

In 1913 Helen took her new political views public with her book *Out of the Dark*. The sweet deaf-blind girl who made the best out of any situation had been replaced by a fighter whose strong opinions on behalf of others shocked a lot of people, including her own conservative southern family. Not only did she stand up for the rights of workers, women who wanted to vote, and other deaf-blind people, she also joined the National Association for the Advancement of Colored People (NAACP) to fight against racial **segregation**. Helen stuck up for anyone who didn't get a fair shot because they were considered different.

The *S* Word

A lot of people talk about socialism now like it's evil, but its basic principle is fairness. The idea is that there shouldn't be rich or poor people. Instead, everyone should share wealth. In socialist countries, the government controls factories and the amount of possessions people get. Helen's views didn't go that far, but she did believe in fairer rights for workers, who during her time often labored ten hours a day, six days a week, without any kind of compensation if they got hurt while on the job.

Helen
Speaks Up

As Helen stood on the stage in front of a crowd gathered to hear her speak in an auditorium in Montclair, New Jersey, her heart seemed to stop beating and her voice choked in her throat. On a cold February day in 1913, she was supposed to give the very first lecture that was part of a big speaking tour. For all the grueling work she'd done to use her voice, she didn't think she could squeak out the first word of her speech, "The Heart and the Hand, or the right use of

our senses."

All these people, whose movements she could feel as they shifted in their seats, had paid good money to hear her speak—money that she and Annie desperately needed to live. She had no other choice than to get on with it, so Helen finally began to talk. Although she was still hard to understand (Annie stayed onstage to interpret), the audience loved hearing all about her hopes, fears, and joys. The lecture tour was a huge success all across the country.

Alas, not everything was going as well as Helen's lectures. Annie and John were having serious troubles in their marriage. They fought all the time. He thought Annie was too involved with Helen; meanwhile she accused him of spending too much money and drinking. In May 1913 John sailed for Europe on a voyage of more than four months without his wife. Absence did not make the heart grow fonder,

Famous Folks Who Came to Hear Helen Speak:

- Electric lightbulb inventor Thomas Edison
- Former president William Howard Taft
- Legendary opera tenor Enrico Caruso
- Ford Motor Company founder Henry Ford

and when he returned, he and Annie fought worse than ever. By 1914, he had moved out of the farmhouse and split from Annie—although they were never formally divorced.

That wasn't Annie's only issue. She started to experience health problems as well. Worried that she wasn't well enough to be Helen's sole guardian and keep up with the organization of their increasingly busy lives, Annie hired Polly Thomson, a Scottish woman who became

Helen's lifelong trusted companion. Annie turned out to be the one who needed Polly's help. Her health continued to go downhill until the summer of 1916, when Annie's doctor said her only chance for surviving was to go to a special clinic in Lake Placid, New York. Polly went along to help aid in Annie's recovery.

It was never easy for Helen to be separated from her dear Annie. The two were as close as could be. But this time, she had someone else to keep her from feeling lonely.

Earlier that year, when Polly had to return to Scotland, Annie had hired another secretary to fill in. His name was Peter Fagan, and he fell in love with Helen. At thirty-six years old, Helen had never been in love, but she fell head over heels for Peter. "His love was a bright sun that shone upon my helplessness and isolation," she wrote. "The sweetness of being loved enchanted me." Although Peter

and Helen wanted to get married, they didn't tell anyone about it. Helen's family wouldn't have approved, because in those days people didn't think those with disabilities should get married.

While Helen was staying with her mother during Annie's trip to Lake Placid, she planned to tell Kate about Peter. Unfortunately, a newspaper got ahold of the news that Peter had applied for a marriage license before she had a chance. Kate practically exploded after seeing the headline that her daughter was about to get married.

Helen issued a public statement denying that she was going to marry Peter, and Kate forbid him to come anywhere near her daughter. That didn't keep the lovebirds from planning to **elope** in an elaborate scheme. While Helen traveled with her mother to her sister Mildred's house in Montgomery, Alabama, Peter planned to

intercept them when they switched from boat to train in Savannah, Georgia. Then he'd take Helen to Florida to get married.

It might have worked, except Peter made the big mistake of reserving passage on the same boat to Georgia as Kate and Helen. When Kate saw the passenger list—and his name on it—she quickly made other plans for getting to Montgomery. She and Helen took the train the entire way.

Peter still refused to give up. He showed up at Helen's sister home in Montgomery and was holding Helen's hand on the porch when Mildred's husband came running out with a gun and finally scared away Peter for good.

CHAPTER TWELVE

Helen's Name in Lights

In 1918 a historian named Francis Trevelyan Miller approached Annie and Helen with an unusual pitch. He wanted to make a movie based on Helen's life. The ladies loved the idea!

The movie, *Deliverance*, was definitely the Hollywood version of Helen's life. Francis spiced up her story so that it would entertain audiences. That included a love scene, supposedly happening in Helen's mind, with her and the ancient hero of the Trojan War,

Ulysses! If that wasn't over-the-top enough, the last scene had Helen leading a procession on a white horse while blowing a trumpet. (Helen played herself at the end of the movie, while a little girl played her as a child and another actress played her at Radcliffe.)

Although *Deliverance* got some positive reviews in newspapers, audiences apparently found the movie just as silly as Helen and Annie did. It tanked when it opened in August 1919.

Despite the money for the movie, Helen and Annie continued to be troubled by financial problems. They had expensive taste in clothes, dogs, travel, and living arrangements. The lecture circuit was good money but tough on Helen. So Helen and Annie did something very surprising for a deaf-blind woman and her teacher: They hit the road in 1920 as vaudeville performers.

Annie and Helen's act wasn't anything crazy. First Annie told the story of Helen as a little

What Is Vaudeville?

Vaudeville, a popular form of entertainment until the 1930s, was a bunch of different acts that made up one show. People turned out to theaters to watch comedians, singers, magicians, acrobats, and anyone else who could keep an audience entertained.

girl and how she taught her to communicate. Then Helen showed how she spelled with her fingers, read lips, and talked. After that, there was a brief question-and-answer session with the audience. They only had to perform twenty minutes in the afternoon and another twenty in the evening—and for that they were paid $2,000.

Not only was it easy money, but Annie and Helen also got to wear the kind of beautiful, intricate floor-length dresses they loved. Plus, Helen basked in the excited, adoring reaction of the audiences day after day and night after night.

Annie, on the other hand, was not a fan of the theater. She found vaudeville and its cast of characters tacky and considered Helen too good for this role. To make matters worse, the bright lights hurt her weakening eyes. Polly often had to stand in for Annie as her health and attitude worsened.

Still, Helen stuck with her routine until 1924. Nothing kept the show from going on, not even when Helen found out her mother had died in 1921. She was just about to go onstage when she got the devastating news. Like a true professional, she went on with her act and no one in the audience could have imagined she had just lost one of the most important people in her life.

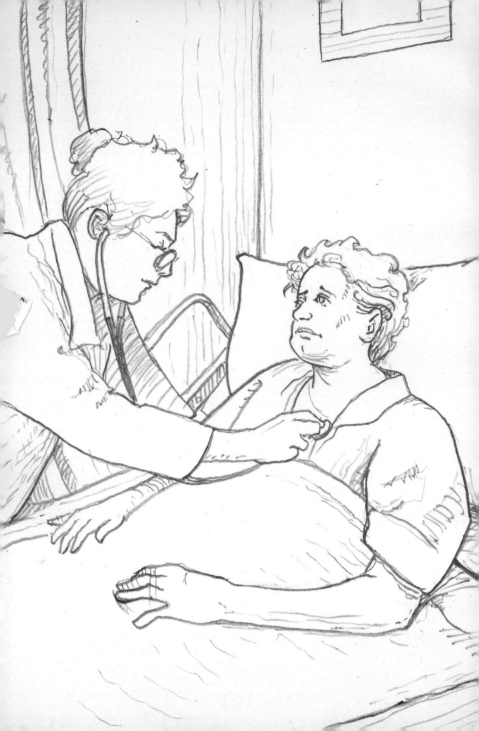

Fairwell,
Teacher

Annie returned from Lake Placid having recovered from her nasty cough, but she never truly got better. Her health got worse and worse until the last several years of her life when she was miserable with physical pain. Not only had she become blind again, but she was also covered in infected **boils** called carbuncles. Despite her terrible condition, Annie never wavered from her devotion to Helen. She continued to accompany her student as they

traveled on fundraising trips for the American Foundation for the Blind.

In 1935 Helen had taken Annie on a trip to Jamaica that she hoped would raise her spirits. When they returned, however, Annie collapsed and was rushed to the hospital, where the doctor said she'd had a heart attack. Helen never left her teacher's side as Annie drifted into a coma from which she'd never awake. On October 20, Annie died at the age of seventy, right next to Helen, where she'd been for nearly fifty years.

Helen wasn't the only one who appreciated how Annie had devoted her life to teaching. Twelve hundred people attended her funeral in New York. To honor her accomplishments, Annie was the first woman laid to rest in the National Cathedral in Washington, D.C., because of her own merits. The bishop in his sermon called Annie, "among the great teachers of all time."

No matter the turnout or public recognition, Helen was completely devastated over the loss of her beloved teacher, the woman who had literally introduced her to the world. She

Teacher

In 1955 Helen paid the ultimate tribute to Annie by publishing a book about her called *Teacher*. Although writing was always hard for Helen, this book might have been the worst. She got insomnia and eczema while working on it. To make matters worse, her first manuscript went up in flames when the house she and Polly lived in had a furnace fire.

needed to find a reason to go on. Helen found it in something that had always driven her: helping others.

Helen had traveled the world for some time raising money for the blind—in the last years of Annie's life, she, Annie, and Polly had been to Yugoslavia, Scotland, England, and Ireland. Everywhere she went, the highest **dignitaries** and the poorest citizens were inspired by her presence and showered her with love and affection. No matter what country, Helen was the ultimate symbol of triumph over adversity.

With Polly by her side, Helen threw herself into her missions as an ambassador of hope with renewed energy and took her biggest trip yet. They traveled to Japan, where after a long journey by ship, they were met by thousands of children waving Japanese and American flags. At a banquet in her honor, Helen met the prime minister, the foreign minister, the mayor of Tokyo, and the country's prince—a bigger reception than any other foreigner had ever received before. She repaid them by going all over the country to deliver ninety-seven lectures in thirty-nine cities, spreading her message that the blind, deaf, and those with other handicaps deserve the same respect as anyone else.

U.S. Tour

The outbreak of World War II put an end to Helen and Polly's travels abroad for a while. But they didn't stay at home. Instead, they went all over the United States, visiting and lifting the spirits of soldiers hurt or blinded in combat.

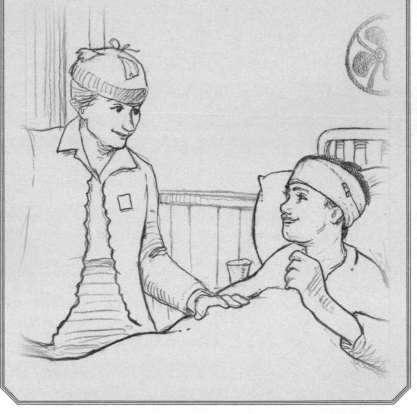

World Tour

After the end of World War II in 1945, and through the 1950s, Helen and Polly zigzagged all over the world even though they were already elderly ladies. Their passports were filled with stamps from:

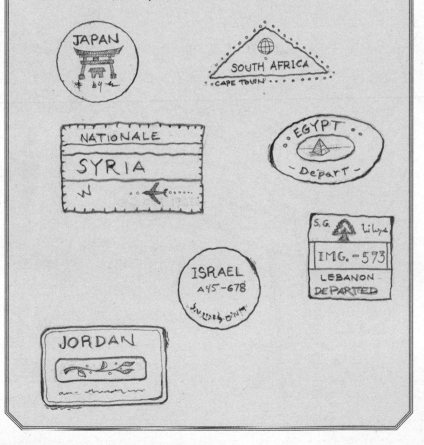

Fighting to the End

While she was alive, Annie had always worried that something would happen to her and Helen would be left alone. That's one of the reasons she hired Polly. But eventually Polly became old as well. On September 26, 1957, Polly suffered a **stroke** while she was in the kitchen of her Connecticut home with Helen, who couldn't call for help. Although it took two and a half hours for the mailman to arrive and call an ambulance, Polly lived. But she never fully recovered, and on March 21, 1960, at the age of seventy-six, she passed away, after spending forty-six years with Helen.

Helen, who by now was nearly eighty years old, had lost her two dearest companions. Still, she found pleasure in life. And the public's fascination with her story never stopped. In fact it only grew after William Gibson wrote a play about Helen's early life. *The Miracle Worker* made its Broadway debut in 1959, starring Anne Bancroft as Annie and child star Patty Duke as Helen. The play had intense scenes that showed how hard it was for Annie to get through to Helen and how much the deaf-blind girl had to overcome. (Both Anne and Patty slapped each other in the face during the show.) Audiences were moved by the play, which became a smash hit. It ran for seven hundred performances on Broadway and was turned into a movie in 1962.

Until she took her last breath on June 1, 1968, at the age of eighty-seven, Helen never stopped learning, fighting for people's rights, and exceeding the expectations of others. It didn't matter that at the end, she could no longer travel around the world, or even leave her home. For Helen, inspiration, hope, strength, and love always lived right inside her: "The best and most beautiful things in the world cannot be seen nor even touched, but just felt in the heart."

10 Things

You Should Know
About Helen Keller

1 An illness Helen contracted before she was two years old caused her to go blind and deaf.

2 Alexander Graham Bell, the inventor of the telephone who met Helen when she was a little girl, stayed friends with her throughout his life.

3 After Helen finally understood the connection between words and the world, when Annie ran her hand under

water while spelling the word for it, she
learned a dozen new words in only a
few hours and hundreds more in the
months to come.

4 When Helen was only eleven years old,
she was accused of plagiarism after
the director of her school printed her
story, which turned out to be just like
one by another author.

5 For a couple of years, Helen attended
one of the top prep schools in the
country, called the Cambridge School
for Young Ladies, where Annie had to
sign all her lectures and many of her
books.

6

Helen graduated from Radcliffe on June 28, 1904, making her the first deaf-blind person in the country to earn a bachelor of arts degree.

7

Once introduced to the world of politics, Helen became a member of the Socialist Party of America and the National Association for the Advancement of Colored People.

8

When Helen was thirty-six years old, she fell in love for the first time with her secretary Peter Fagan, but her family didn't approve and ran him off.

Medal of
Freedom

9 Helen traveled all over the world to advocate for people with disabilities, raise money for the blind, and inspire everyone.

10 In 1964, a few years before Helen passed away, President Lyndon Johnson awarded her the Presidential Medal of Freedom, the country's highest civilian honor.

10 MORE Things

That Are Pretty Cool to Know

1 Whenever Helen was photographed, Annie made sure that her picture was only taken from the right side because her left eye stuck out from her head and made her look blind.

2 Helen learned how to write with paper and pencil by using a ruler as a guide to keep her letters straight. It was such hard work, she often ended her letters by writing, "I am too tired to write more."

3 Helen could play chess! She had a special chessboard where the white pieces were a little bigger than the black ones so she could tell them apart.

4 Although *The Story of My Life* wasn't a bestseller when it came out, it's a book that has withstood the test of time—and culture. Over the last century, it's been translated into over fifty languages!

5 Helen had an operation to remove both her eyes and replace them with blue glass ones because she and Annie didn't think she should appear in public with her protruding left eye. They kept her fake eyes a secret.

6 During her 1937 trip to Japan, Helen became the first woman allowed to touch the Great Buddha of Kamakura, a huge statue of Buddha that weighs ninety–three tons!

7 While in South Africa, Helen received an honorary name from the Zulu tribe—*Homvuselelo*—which means "you have aroused the consciousness of many."

2003
Alabama
quarter

8 Helen met with all the presidents of the United States from Grover Cleveland to Lyndon Johnson. President Franklin Delano Roosevelt once said, "Anything Helen Keller is for, I am for."

9 Between 1946 and 1957, Helen and Polly traveled to five continents and thirty–five countries—including a 40,000–mile tour of Asia.

10 Helen was the first woman ever to receive an honorary degree from Harvard, which she got when she was almost seventy–five!

Glossary

Autobiography: a book in which the author tells the story of his or her life

Boil: a painful swelling on or under the skin

Confederate: a supporter of the group of eleven states that declared independence from the rest of the United States just before the Civil War

Dignitary: a person who holds a position of honor

Editor: someone whose job is to edit writing before it is published

Elope: to run away and get married

Memoir: a story from one's personal experience

Penicillin: the first antibiotic; made from a mold called penicillium that kills bacteria and helps fight disease

Prominent: famous or important

Publicity: information about a person or an event that is given out to get the public's attention or approval

Segregation: the act or practice of keeping people or groups apart

Stroke: a sudden lack of oxygen in part of the brain caused by the blocking or breaking of a blood vessel

Places to Visit

Reach out, either online or in real life, to some of the places from Helen Keller's amazing life.

Helen Keller's Birthplace, Tuscumbia, Alabama
helenkellerbirthplace.org

Perkins School for the Blind, Watertown, Massachusetts
The oldest school for the blind in the U.S.
perkins.org

National Cathedral, Washington, D.C.
Helen, Annie, and Polly were all laid to rest in the columbarium of St. Joseph's Chapel on the crypt level.
nationalcathedral.org

Helen Keller's Kids Museum Online
braillebug.org/hkmuseum.asp

Bibliography

Helen Keller: Courage in Darkness, Emma
   Carlson Berne, Sterling Publishing Co.,
   2009.

Helen Keller: Her Life in Pictures, George
   Sullivan, Scholastic Nonfiction, 2007.

Helen Keller: Selected Writings, New York
   University Press, 2005.

The Story of My Life, Helen Keller,
   Doubleday, 1903.

To Love This Life: Quotations by Helen Keller,
   American Foundation for the Blind, 2000.

Who Was Helen Keller?, Gare Thompson,
   Grosset & Dunlap, 2003.

*The World at Her Fingertips: The Story of
   Helen Keller*, Joan Dash, Scholastic Press,
   2002.

Index

A
Adams, John, 14
Anagnos, Michael, 9, 11, 53, 57

B
Bell, Alexander Graham, 26–28, 114
braille, 51, 52
Bridgman, Laura, 28, 38

C
Cambridge School for Young Ladies, 67–68, 115
Cleveland, Grover, 54, 55, 121

D
deaf-blind people, 27–28, 73, 79, 84
deaf people
communication, 38–39, 43–49
education for, 27–28
Deliverance (movie), 11, 97–98
disabled people, rights of, 8, 93

F
Fagan, Peter, 9, 11, 91–95, 116

G
Gilman, Arthur, 67–68, 70, 71

H
Harvard, 62, 121

J
Johnson, Lyndon, 117, 121

K
Keller, Captain Arthur, 8
background, 13
death, 10
Keller, Helen, 8, 10–11
awards and honors, 107, 117, 120, 121
beliefs and philosophy, 6–7, 113
birth, 13
childhood, 4, 14–23, 34–37, 40–41
college education and degrees, 10, 73–76, 79, 116, 121
death, 113
education, 9, 10, 11, 23, 61–62, 65, 67–71, 115–116
fame, 53–58, 100
illness, 14–17
loss of sight and hearing, 16–17, 114
movies and plays about, 97–98
personality traits, 6, 20–21
political views, 83–85, 116
romance, 91–95, 116

senses, 4, 6
speaking ability, 4, 56,
    87–89
travels, 61, 63–65, 103–104,
    106–109, 117, 120, 121
writings, 4, 49, 57–59,
    76–78, 81, 105, 115,
    118, 119
Keller, Kate, 8
background, 14
death, 10, 101
Keller, Mildred, 21, 23, 93, 95

L
Ladies Home Journal, 76,
    77–78

M
Macy, John Albert, 9, 11,
    77–78, 81–83, 89–90
Miracle Worker, The (play),
    11, 112

N
New York City, 61, 65

O
Out of the Dark, 84

P
Perkins Institution, 11, 27–
    28, 31, 33, 38, 53, 56, 59
plagiarism, 58, 115

R
Radcliffe College, 10, 62, 67,
    73, 98, 116
Rockefeller, John D., 65
Roosevelt, Franklin Delano,
    121

S
sign language, 38–39, 43–49
socialism, 85
Socialist Party of America,
    83, 116
Story of My Life, The, 78
Sullivan, Annie, 9
arrival in Helen's home, 10,
    24–25, 32–36
behavior, 35–37, 40–41
childhood and education,
    29–31
death, 10, 104–105
health problems, 90–91,
    100, 103
relationship with Helen, 8,
    9, 49, 81–82
romance and marriage, 9,
    81–83, 89–90
separation from Helen,
    70–71
travels with Helen, 61, 63–
    65, 68–69, 103–104

T
Thomson, Polly, 9
friendship with Helen, 9,
    90–91
stroke and death, 11,
    111–112
travels with Helen, 107,
    108–109, 121

V
vaudeville, 10, 99

W
women, education for, 62
women's right to vote, 83
Wright-Humason School for
    the Deaf, 11, 61, 67

Also Available:

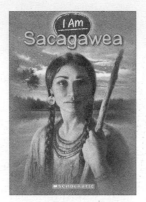

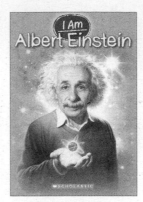